Little Golden Books

Published in the United States by Golden Books, an imprint of Random House
Children's Books, a division of Random House, Inc., 1745 Broadway, New York,
NY 10019, and in Canada by Random House of Canada Limited, Toronto.
Golden Books, A Golden Book, A Little Golden Book, the G colophon,
and the distinctive gold spine are registered trademarks of Random House, Inc.
Nickelodeon, Bubble Guppies, Dora the Explorer, SpongeBob SquarePants,
Team Umizoomi, and all related titles, logos, and characters are trademarks
of Viacom International Inc. The stories contained in this work were
originally published separately by Golden Books as follows:
*Dora's Fairytale Adventure,* in 2011, adapted by Molly Reisner and illustrated by
David Aikins, based on the screenplay "King Unicornio" by Rosemary Contreras;
*Sponge in Space!,* in 2012, adapted by Geof Smith and illustrated by Heather Martinez,
based on the screenplay "Sandy's Rocket" by Sherm Cohen, Aaron Springer, and
Peter Burns; *It's Time for Bubble Puppy!,* in 2012, illustrated by Eren Blanquet Unten,
based on the screenplay "Bubble Puppy!" by Jonny Belt, Robert Scull, and Adam
Peltzman; *Dora's Birthday Surprise!,* in 2010, by Molly Reisner and illustrated by David
Aikins; *Top of the Class!,* in 2011, by James Killeen and illustrated by Heather Martinez;
*Find the Dinosaurs!,* in 2012, illustrated by Chris George and David Aikins, based on the
screenplay "The Dinosaur Museum Mishap" by Brian L. Perkins and Jeff Borkin;
*The Big Ballet Show,* in 2012, illustrated by John Loter and Brenda Goddard, based on
the screenplay "Dora's Ballet Adventure" by Teri Weiss; *Mr. FancyPants!,* in 2009,
adapted by Geof Smith and illustrated by Caleb Meurer, based on the screenplay
"To SquarePants or Not To" by Luke Brookshier, Nate Cash, and Steven Banks; and
*Roller Rintoo!,* in 2010, adapted by Geof Smith and illustrated by Jason Fruchter,
based on the screenplay "Roller Rintoo" by Chris Nee.

SpongeBob created by

*Stephen Hillenburg*

randomhouse.com/kids

Educators and librarians, for a variety of teaching tools, visit us at
randomhouse.com/teachers

ISBN: 978-0-375-85120-9

PRINTED IN CHINA

10 9 8 7 6 5 4 3 2 1

# a Little Golden Book® Collection

## nickelodeon™

# Tales

A GOLDEN BOOK • NEW YORK

# Contents

Dora and the Unicorn King • 1
Adapted by Molly Reisner   Illustrated by David Aikins
Based on the teleplay "King Unicornio" by Rosemary Contreras

Sponge in Space! • 25
Adapted by Geof Smith   Illustrated by Heather Martinez
Based on the screenplay "Sandy's Rocket"
by Sherm Cohen, Aaron Springer, and Peter Burns

It's Time for Bubble Puppy! • 49
Illustrated by Eren Blanquet Unten
Based on the screenplay by Jonny Belt, Robert Scull, and Adam Peltzman

Dora's Birthday Surprise! • 73
By Molly Reisner
Illustrated by David Aikins

Top of the Class! • 97
By James Killeen   Illustrated by Heather Martinez

Find the Dinosaurs! • 121
Illustrated by Chris George and Dave Aikins
Based on the screenplay "The Dinosaur Museum Mishap"
by Brian L. Perkins and Jeff Borkin

The Big Ballet Show • 145
Adapted by Geof Smith
Illustrated by John Loter and Brenda Goddard
Based on the screenplay "Dora's Ballet Adventure" by Teri Weiss

Mr. FancyPants! • 169
Adapted by Geof Smith   Illustrated by Caleb Meuer
Based on the screenplay "To Square or Not To"
by Luke Brookshier, Nate Cash, and Steven Banks

Roller Rintoo! • 193
Adapted by Geof Smith   Illustrated by Jason Fruchter
Based on the teleplay "Roller Rintoo" by Chris Nee

nickelodeon

Dora the Explorer

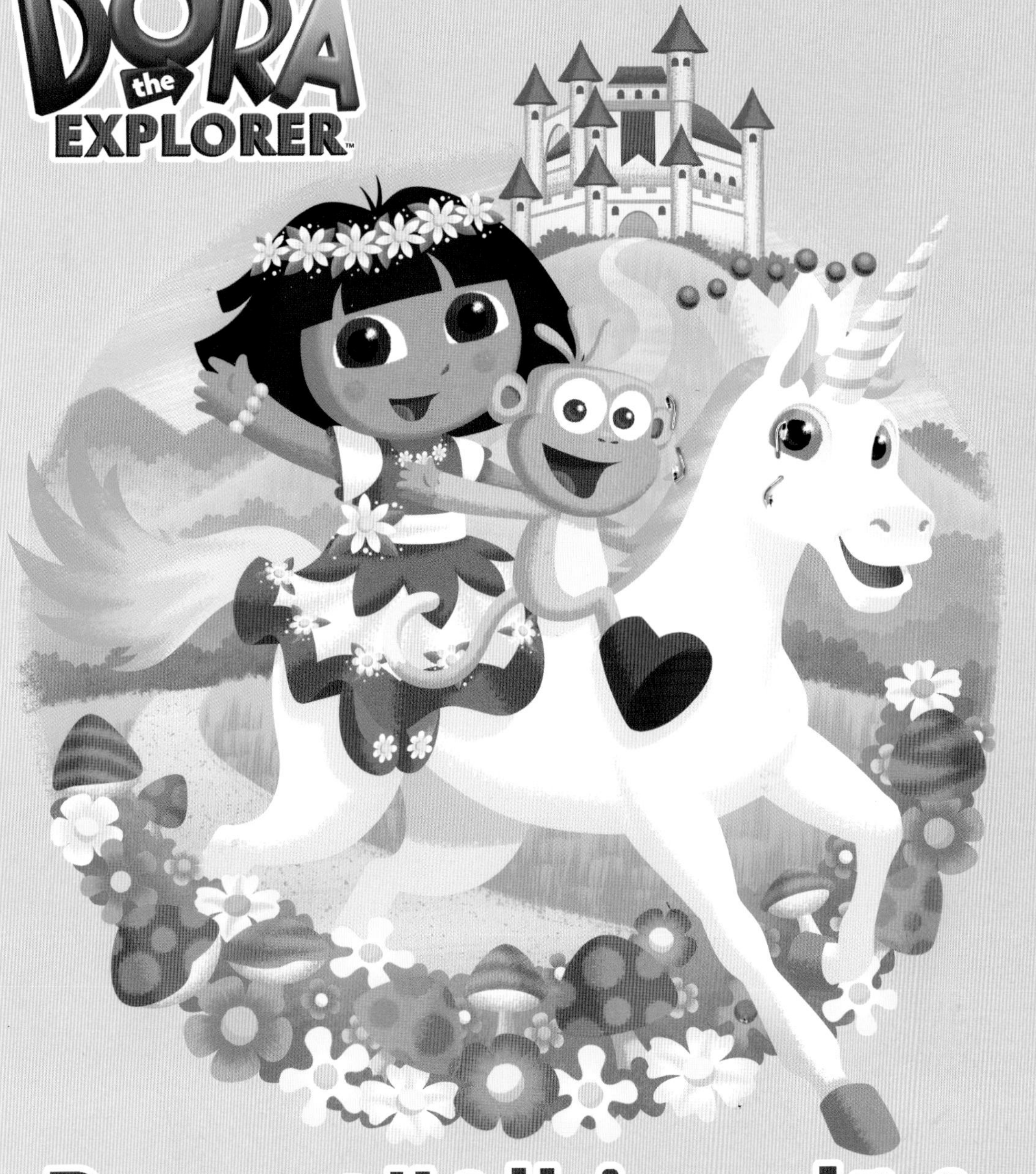

# Dora and the Unicorn King

**W**hile walking through the forest one day, Dora and Boots saw a big, beautiful rainbow in the sky. Suddenly, their friend Unicornio came racing down the side! He was giving his friends a ride.

A rabbit holding a scroll hopped up to Unicornio.

"'Because you are kind, strong, smart, and brave, the citizens of the forest have picked you to be king,'" the rabbit read. "'You must get to the Castle in the Enchanted Forest so you can be crowned!'"

Unicornio was worried. He didn't think he was kind, strong, smart, or brave.

Dora hugged Unicornio. "Boots and I will show you that you are all those things!"

The three friends journeyed to the beautiful Enchanted Forest.

"How will we find the Castle?" Boots asked.
"Let's ask Map!" said Dora.
Map said that they had to go through the Riddle Tree, then past the Volcano. Then they would see the Castle.

On the way to the Riddle Tree, the friends met five elves picking peaches. All the elves had peaches in their baskets . . . except Littlest Elf. He stretched and jumped, but he couldn't reach a peach!

"Want a boost?" Unicornio asked.

The little elf climbed up Unicornio's neck. Now he could reach lots of peaches!

"Thank you," said Littlest Elf. "You're very kind."

The other elves agreed. Unicornio was happy to discover that he WAS kind!

Dora, Boots, and Unicornio traveled on.
They finally found the Riddle Tree. An owl sat
on one of its branches.

"No one is as smart as I!" bragged Owl. He
challenged Unicornio to a riddle contest.

The Riddle Tree asked, "Who lives in a castle and rules over all that can be seen—"

"A king!" interrupted Owl. But he was wrong.

"A ruler is not always a king," the Riddle Tree said. "Sometimes she's a . . ."

Unicornio took a moment to think.

"A queen!" Unicornio answered. He was right! "You're really smart," said Owl.

Just then, a golden tunnel opened up in the Riddle Tree's trunk! Unicornio, Dora, and Boots waved goodbye and entered the tunnel.

At the end of the tunnel, the friends found the Volcano. The Volcano rumbled. Puffs of smoke rose from the top . . . and a dragon flew out!

As Boots was running away from the
dragon, he tripped on a rock!

"Uh-oh, the dragon is going to get Boots!"
cried Dora. Unicornio remembered that he had
a special way to protect his friends.

Unicornio stood in front of Dora and Boots.
"My magic horn will keep the dragon back!"
he said. He stomped his hooves, and magic
sparkles came out of his horn!

Dora and Boots helped by stomping, too.
The sparkles made a powerful shield.

The dragon bounced off the shield and flew away!

"Unicornio, thanks for protecting me," said Boots. "You're so brave!"

Unicornio was very proud that he had helped his friends.

Dora could see the Castle in the distance.
She and Boots climbed onto Unicornio's back.
He galloped as fast as he could.

Unicornio had already proved to himself that he was kind, smart, and brave. But he still had to prove that he was strong. Only then would Unicornio feel ready to be crowned king!

On the way to the Castle, Rabbit stopped Unicornio. "I need your help! Squirrel fell into the water!" he cried.

Unicornio raced as fast as he could along the riverbank to save Squirrel. But the water was rushing too quickly!

"We need something to help pull Squirrel out of the water," said Boots.

Dora checked Backpack and found the perfect thing—a life preserver! She threw the ring around Squirrel.

"We're going to have to be super strong!" yelled Dora.

"I'm strong!" Unicornio said, and he tied the rope around his body.

Unicornio pulled and pulled . . . and finally
pulled Squirrel out of the water to safety!

The forest creatures cheered.
"You're really strong! Thanks for helping me!"
said Squirrel.

All the fairies, elves, and animals of the Enchanted Forest arrived at the Castle wearing their finest clothes. They thanked Unicornio for being kind, smart, brave, and strong.

Dora was very proud of Unicornio.

"Now do you see that you are ready to be king?" she asked.

"Yes," Unicornio said. "I AM ready!"

"I now declare you king!" announced Rabbit, putting a crown on Unicornio's head. Trumpets tooted and everyone celebrated.

Dora and Boots cheered, "Hip, hip, hooray for King Unicornio!"

One day, SpongeBob went to visit his friend Sandy. When SpongeBob got to the Treedome, he couldn't believe his eyes.

Sandy had a rocket!

"I'm going to the moon tomorrow,"
Sandy said.

SpongeBob asked if he could go, too.
"I want to see aliens—and I don't take up
much room."

"Sure, you can come on the space trip
with me, SpongeBob," Sandy replied. "But
there are no aliens on the moon."

That night, SpongeBob was too excited
to sleep. He couldn't stop thinking about
his trip to outer space the next day.

SpongeBob would steer the speeding rocket up into space, zooming past stars and comets.

And he would boldly explore strange planets.

SpongeBob didn't believe what Sandy
had said about aliens. He knew he would
meet bizarre beings on the moon.
    "I'm not scared of aliens," SpongeBob
told himself. "There are strange creatures
everywhere."

Suddenly, Patrick popped through SpongeBob's window.

"I heard about your trip, SpongeBob," said Patrick. "We have to make Sandy's rocket alien-proof."

SpongeBob thought that was an excellent idea.

SpongeBob gave Patrick a tour of the rocket.
Patrick was amazed.

"I wonder which button makes the rocket go,"
the sea star said.

"This one," replied SpongeBob.

The rocket **RUMBLED**. Flames shot
from its engine. The rocket began to
rise higher and higher into the sky.

The rocket went faster and faster as it flew into space. Suddenly, SpongeBob and Patrick were weightless.

"Wow!" exclaimed SpongeBob. "What a weird feeling! It's like we're swimming, but it's floatier!"

The rocket headed for the moon, missed it, and sped back to Earth.

SpongeBob and Patrick landed with a **THUD**. "Who turned the heavy back on?" groaned Patrick.

But SpongeBob and Patrick didn't realize that
the rocket had landed back in Bikini Bottom.
They thought they were on the moon!
"Wow, this looks like home," Patrick said.
"No. It's a trick," whispered SpongeBob. "We
must explore! But we have to be very careful. . . .

"We found an alien!" exclaimed SpongeBob. "Look at its tentacles . . . its giant fleshy head . . . its huge nose! It's horrible! We have to capture it and bring it back to Earth."

SpongeBob threw a net
over the alien.
"I'll prove to Sandy that
aliens *do* exist," he said.

Just then, Sandy appeared. "What are you doing, SpongeBob?" she asked.

SpongeBob gulped. "That alien is pretending to be Sandy! It even knows my name!

"The aliens are reading our thoughts and trying to control our minds!" he warned Patrick. "They're tricky—but we have nets!"

SpongeBob and Patrick captured Sandy.

They got Mr. Krabs.

And they netted Mrs. Puff and Gary.
Soon they had caught everyone in Bikini Bottom.

When they were finished, Patrick realized something. "If the aliens can trick us," he said to SpongeBob, "how do I know you're really you and I'm really me?"

SpongeBob and Patrick grabbed their nets and stared at each other suspiciously.

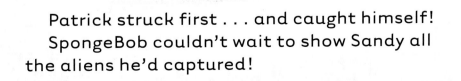

Patrick struck first . . . and caught himself!
SpongeBob couldn't wait to show Sandy all
the aliens he'd captured!

"Next stop: Bikini Bottom!" exclaimed
SpongeBob.

The rocket shot into space again, but
this time it ran out of fuel. It sputtered
and wheezed . . . and landed on the moon!

"SpongeBob, we 'aliens' want to have a word with you," said Sandy.

"Does anyone know how to fix rockets?" asked SpongeBob.

One morning, Gil was on his way to school when he heard barking.

"I hear puppies!" he said.

Gil followed the barks and found a whole *bunch* of puppies!

"These puppies are up for adoption," explained a friendly lady snail. "That means we're looking for people to take them home and give them nice places to live."

"I wish I had a puppy like that one," Gil said, pointing to a cute little guy with orange spots that was barking happily. The puppy was friendly—and really good at chasing bubbles!

When Gil got to school, he told his friends Molly, Goby, Oona, Deema, and Nonny all about the puppy. "I wish I could adopt him," he said.

"Adopting a pet is a great thing to do," said
their teacher, Mr. Grouper. "You just have to
find the right pet for you."

"I want a cat that says *meow*," said Molly.

"I want a parrot!" said Deema.

"I like guinea pigs!" said Goby.

"I think that puppy would be perfect for me," Gil said. "We'd be best buddies. He'd lick my face to wake me up every morning, and we would run and play in the park all the time!"

"But Gil, you can't play with
the puppy all the time," Molly said.
"You have to take care of him, too."

"That's right," Mr. Grouper said.
"Taking care of a pet is a really big job."

"If your puppy is hungry, you'll have to give it food to eat," Mr. Grouper said.

"And puppies get thirsty, too, so they
need lots of water," said Molly.

"And when your puppy needs to go outside," said Goby, "you'll put him on a leash and take him for a walk!"

"If that puppy was my pet, I would take really good care of him," said Gil.

"You would?" said Mr. Grouper. "Well, then, come with me. Everybody, let's line up. I have something to show you!"

Mr. Grouper led the class through their
watery world. Finally, they arrived at the
puppy adoption center!

"This is where I met that puppy!" said Gil.

But when Gil looked for the puppies, they were all gone!

The lady snail told him that all the puppies had been adopted—including Gil's favorite! Gil was very sad.

"Here, you'll need these," said the lady snail,
handing Gil a bowl and a leash.
"But why?" asked Gil.

"Because he's coming back to class with us!" said Mr. Grouper. "We adopted him!"

*"Arf! Arf!"* barked the happy little puppy.

All the Bubble Guppies cheered. "Yay! Thank you, Mr. Grouper!"

Everyone was very excited about their new pet.

They all agreed to help
take care of the new puppy.

"I'll give him
baths," said Gil.

"And I'll take him out for walks," said Goby.

Molly and Nonny couldn't wait to feed the puppy and give him water.

Oona said she would train the puppy.

"And I'll hug him!" promised Deema.

"But what should we call him?" asked Molly.

*"Arf!"* barked the puppy, and a big bubble came out of his mouth!

"I know," said Gil. "Let's call him . . . BUBBLE PUPPY!"

Everyone thought Bubble Puppy was a wonderful
name. They all took turns hugging Bubble Puppy, and
he licked them all back.

Gil gave Bubble Puppy a really big hug. "I'm glad we adopted you, boy," he said.

"*Arf!*" barked Bubble Puppy. He was happy to have a nice new home with all his new friends, the Bubble Guppies.

nickelodeon

# DORA the EXPLORER™

# Dora's Birthday Surprise!

¡*Hola!* I'm Dora, and this is my best friend, Boots. Today is a day that only comes once a year—my birthday!

Look! Silly Mail Bird has a message for me. Let's read it together.

Dear Dora,
¡feliz cumpleaños! Happy birthday!
Get ready for your Birthday Scavenger Hunt! We have a present for you, but you'll have to look for three clues to find it. We'll all celebrate together when you find the last clue.
Love,
Mami and Papi

A scavenger hunt! *¡Fantástico!* Will you help me look for clues? Great!

I wonder where we should start looking. Who do we ask for help when we don't know which way to go? *¡Sí!* Map!

Map says that the first clue is in the tallest tree in the Nutty Forest. The second clue is at Troll Bridge. And the third clue is on top of Rainbow Rock. *¡Vámonos!* Let's go!

Hey! There's Tico! Tico says he'll give us a ride to the Nutty Forest. *¡Gracias, amigo!* Thanks!

We made it to the Nutty Forest! Now, which tree is the tallest?

Yeah, the tree in the middle is the tallest! *¡Excelente!*

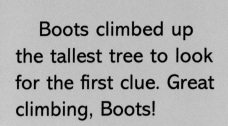

Boots climbed up
the tallest tree to look
for the first clue. Great
climbing, Boots!

There's a box hanging from a branch. Help Boots climb to the branch. *¡Sube, sube!* Climb, climb!

There's a ball of yarn inside the box! The yarn is my first clue. Let's look for the next one.

We need to go to Troll Bridge for the second clue. But first we have to get through the Purple Gate. Will you check Backpack for something that will open the lock? Say "Backpack!"

"Do you see anything that will open the lock?

Yeah, that's right, the purple key! *¡Muy bien!*"

We're at Troll Bridge! The Grumpy Old Troll says we have to solve his riddle to get the box. Will you help?

*"This dessert is sweet
And a birthday treat to eat.
But first it needs to bake.
It's a birthday . . ."*

Hmm. What's a sweet dessert you
bake and eat on a birthday? *¡Sí!* A CAKE!

Uh-oh! Swiper wants to swipe the box that's holding my second birthday clue!

He says he won't swipe my box because it's my birthday. *¡Gracias, Swiper!*

Now let's see what's inside the box. It's a little bowl! The first clue was a ball of yarn, and the second clue is a bowl. I wonder what my present is. Let's go find the last clue at Rainbow Rock!

*¡Mira!* Look! There are stars everywhere!
Artista, the Skywriting Explorer Star, wrote
a birthday message for me in the sky!

How many stars do you see? *Uno, dos, tres, cuatro, cinco, seis, siete, ocho, nueve, diez.* Ten stars! We need to reach up and catch the stars. Reach high in the air!

Super catching!

We're at Rainbow Rock! To get to the top, we need to climb the colored rocks. Do you see them?

Call out the color of each rock to show us which way to go! Red! Orange! Yellow! Green! Blue! Purple! *¡Fantástico!*

We made it to the top! Do you see a box
hidden anywhere? There's a box in that bush.
Let's open it to find the last clue!

The third clue is a carton of milk! What are all the clues, again? Yarn, a bowl, and milk. What do you think Mami and Papi got me? I have an idea. . . . I really hope I'm right! Let's find out at my party!

Yay! All my friends and family are at my birthday party. Mmm, Papi made a chocolate cake! I'm making a wish before I blow out my candles. What will you wish for on your birthday?

*¡Mira!* I was right! Mami and Papi gave me a kitten—just like I thought the clues were telling me! I'm going to name him Gatito. He loves playing with the yarn and drinking milk from his bowl!

Thanks for helping me find the birthday clues and for coming to my party! *¡Gracias!*

Business was booming at the Krusty Krab. "Hurry up with those Krabby Patties!" yelled the owner, Mr. Krabs.

"I'm a Krabby Patty machine!" replied the fry cook, SpongeBob, who was working harder than ever to fill the many orders.

Plankton, the evil owner of the Chum Bucket restaurant, watched from across the street.

"They have so many customers!" he exclaimed. "I must steal the secret Krabby Patty formula and put the Krusty Krab out of business—once and for all!"

So Plankton created a wonderfully evil plan. It started with a disguise. . . .

The next day, a tiny green salesman visited Mr. Krabs.

"Boy, do I have a deal for you, Mr. Krabs. This machine can make five thousand Krabby Patties a day."

"And you can try it out for FREE!" the salesman promised. "Just send your head fry cook to my school."

"FREE? You've got a deal!" said Mr. Krabs.

Plankton's plan was working perfectly. Now he just had to trick SpongeBob into giving him the Krabby Patty formula.

"Take this textbook, Mr. SquarePants," instructed Plankton. "Classes in pattyology begin tomorrow morning!"

"A master's degree in pattyology!
Textbooks! HOMEWORK!" cried SpongeBob.
"I LOVE SCHOOL!"

# What is the Krabby Patty Formula?

SpongeBob arrived at school bright and early the next day.

"Who would like to answer the question on the board?" asked Plankton.

"Me, ME, **ME!**" shouted SpongeBob.

"This is going to be harder than I thought,"
Plankton grumbled to himself.

"That's enough classwork," said Plankton. "How would you like to try out the Krabby Pattinator Five Thousand?"

"ARE YOU KIDDING?" screamed SpongeBob.

"Mr. SquarePants, please gather the Krabby
Patty ingredients for me," said Plankton.

"Oh, I've already loaded the machine with
the ingredients. I also woke up early and read
the whole manual," declared SpongeBob.

"Let's make sure the mixture is correct," Plankton said, peering into the Krabby Patty machine. "Ah. Here we go!"

"Go?" said SpongeBob, hitting the Start button.

"Nooo!" yelled Plankton as he fell into the Krabby Pattinator 5000.

Plankton was not pleased.

"That's it! This isn't worth it! Class dismissed . . . FOREVER!"
Plankton pressed a button and the Krabby Pattinator 5000 blew to pieces.

SpongeBob was dejected. His dreams of school had been shattered!

"No classes! No homework! And worst of all, NO GRADUATION!"

Back at work, SpongeBob's job suddenly
seemed pointless. He could barely flip a single
patty. Mr. Krabs wished he'd gotten his free
machine. But even more, he missed having his
speedy fry cook.

"SpongeBob is the best fry cook ever to flip for the Krusty Krab—and he's better than any machine!" declared Mr. Krabs. Suddenly, Mr. Krabs had a plan.

"Mr. Squidward, get to work inviting all
of SpongeBob's friends here tomorrow!"
"Why?" Squidward mumbled.
"Just do it!" Mr. Krabs shouted.

"Congratulations, SpongeBob! Based on your outstanding performance in the Krusty Krab kitchen, you have earned the first-ever degree in **FRY COOK MASTERY,**" announced Mr. Krabs.

SpongeBob was happy to be a master of fry cook arts. And he was even happier to have the best friends in Bikini Bottom!

**M**illi, Geo, and their best robot friend, Bot, are Team Umizoomi—the tiniest super heroes ever! When someone has a problem in Umi City, the team uses its Mighty Math Powers to help solve it!

123

Geo and Milli were excited. They were going to the Dinosaur Museum with kids from Umi City.

"Let's play dinosaurs," Milli said.

"ROAR!" growled Geo.

Suddenly, the Umi Alarm sounded!

"That means someone needs our help!" said Milli.

"We can see who it is on my Belly, Belly, Bellyscreen!" announced Bot.

It was Mouse. He lived at the museum and helped take care of the dinosaurs.

"A big thunderstorm scared Stegosaurus, Brachiosaurus, and Microraptor," said Mouse. "They all ran away from the museum! The storm is over—but the dinosaurs are lost in Umi City!"

"Oh, no!" said Milli. "We have to find the dinosaurs and take them back to the museum, where they belong."

"We can use our Mighty Math Powers!"
Milli exclaimed. "I can make any pattern
with my Pattern Power!"

"I can build anything with my Super
Shapes," Geo said.

"And I can show you anything on my
Bellyscreen," Bot said.

"We can take UmiCar to the museum," Geo said. "Seat belts on! Go, UmiCar!"

At the Dinosaur Museum, Mouse gave Team Umizoomi some cards that told them what they needed to know to find each dinosaur. The team looked at the cards on Bot's Super Robot Computer.

The computer said that the Brachiosaurus had a really long neck. In fact, he was one of the tallest dinosaurs.

"Where should we look to find the tall Brachiosaurus?" Geo asked.

"We'll have to look very high," Bot said.

Team Umizoomi looked all around Umi City. They searched the tops of the tall buildings.

Suddenly, Geo shouted, "There's Brachiosaurus! He's going into the movie theater!"

It was really dark in the theater, so Geo
used his Super Shapes to make a flashlight.
"I need two trapezoids and three
rectangles," he said. *"Super Shapes!"*

"Umirrific!" Milli cheered.
"What a super flashlight!"

Team Umizoomi searched the dark
theater with the flashlight.

"There's Brachiosaurus!" they shouted.
"Good thing we found him," Milli said.
"Dinosaurs sure don't belong in the city."
"Thanks for finding me, Team Umizoomi!"
said Brachiosaurus. "I was scared all alone
in the dark!"

Team Umizoomi showed Brachiosaurus
how to get back to the Dinosaur Museum.
They still had two more dinosaurs to find.

"My robot computer says that Stegosauruses have plates on their backs," Bot reported. "They also like to eat plants and leaves."

"I know where there are lots of plants and leaves," Milli said. "In the park!"

Team Umizoomi raced to the park and looked for Stegosaurus. He was stuck in a boat in the middle of the big pond!

Milli told Stegosaurus to paddle to shore with his tail. Bot's robot computer calculated that Stegosaurus needed to paddle twelve times. Team Umizoomi helped him count.

"Thanks for the great counting, Team Umizoomi!" said Stegosaurus. "I couldn't have done it without your help!"

Bot showed Stegosaurus how to get back to the Dinosaur Museum. Milli waved goodbye. "See you later, Stegosaurus!"

Team Umizoomi had rescued two lost dinosaurs. They only needed to find one more—Microraptor.

Bot's robot computer told Team Umizoomi that Microraptors were very small dinosaurs. They liked to climb to high places and glide through the air.

Milli, Geo, and Bot raced to the tallest building in Umi City.

There was an elevator to take them to the top of the building, but one of the buttons was missing.

"We can use my Pattern Power to fix it," Milli said. "The pattern goes pink, blue, pink, blue, pink. What color comes next? Right! Blue!"

Team Umizoomi found Microraptor at the top of the building! Now they had to get back to the Dinosaur Museum quickly.

"I'll take us there!" said Microraptor. "Hop on my back and I'll give you a ride!"

Microraptor spread his wings and took off.

"Sizzling circuits!" Bot exclaimed. "We're gliding!"

Team Umizoomi did it! They got all the dinosaurs back to the Dinosaur Museum just in time for the kids to see them. Brachiosaurus, Stegosaurus, and Microraptor were all very happy to be home.

"I feel a celebration coming on!" said
Bot. Everybody started to dance.
"With our Mighty Math Powers, we can
do anything!" Milli cheered.

**DORA** the **EXPLORER**

# The Big Ballet Show

It was the day of the big Dance Show. Dora and her friends were getting ready backstage. Everyone was very excited. They all loved to dance.

"Are you ready to start the show?" Boots asked Dora.

"Almost," she replied. "We're just waiting for the Delivery Duck to bring our dance slippers from the Dance School."

Suddenly, the Delivery Duck flew into the room with a box.

Dora quickly opened the box and looked inside. "Oh, no!" she cried. "These aren't dance slippers! These are scuba flippers! We can't dance in these."

Dora and Boots told the other dancers
they would run to the Dance School
and get the slippers.

"We'll be back in time to start the Dance Show," Dora said. Everyone wished her luck.

"How will we find the Dance School?" Boots asked.

"Let's ask Map!" said Dora.

Map said that to reach the Dance School, they had to go through Bunny Hop Hill and Benny's Barn.

Dora and Boots ran and ran until they came to Bunny Hop Hill. There was a door in the hill, but it didn't have a knob.

"How are we going to open the door?" Boots asked.

Luckily, a helpful bunny hopped up to them.

"You need to go through three doors to get through Bunny Hop Hill," the bunny said. "To open them, you have to play Follow the Bunny. Just do what I do!"

Dora and Boots hopped like the bunny to open the first door.

They shook their bunny tails to open the second door.

To open the third door, they wiggled their ears like the bunny.

Dora and Boots opened all the doors and
made it through Bunny Hop Hill. After thanking
the bunny, they ran to Benny's Barn.

"Hi, Benny," Dora said. "We need to pass through your barn to go to the Dance School and get our dance slippers."

"No problem, Dora," replied Benny. "And guess what? You're just in time for the Animal Dance Hoedown!

"To get through the barn, you have to dance like an animal," Benny said.

"Jump like a frog!

"Gallop like a horse!

"And flap your arms
like a chicken!"

"We made it through Benny's Barn," Dora
said. "Now we have to run to the Dance School
and get those slippers!"

Dora and Boots finally reached the Dance School—but the front gate was locked!

"How will we open the gate?" Boots asked.

"There must be a key to unlock it," Dora replied. "Let's try to find it."

Dora spotted some keys hanging from a branch. She was about to take them when Swiper jumped out from behind the tree. He wanted to swipe the keys!

"Swiper, no swiping!" Dora and Boots said.

"Oh, mannn!" Swiper said, and gave Dora the keys.

Dora opened the gate, went into the school, and found the box of dance slippers. But it was almost time for the Dance Show! How would she and Boots get back in time?

Suddenly, the Dance Train rolled by and offered them a ride!

The Dance Train raced quickly along the tracks. Dora and Boots were at the Dance Show in no time.

When they arrived with the box of slippers, the other dancers cheered. "¡Fantástico! Dora and Boots saved the Dance Show!"

Everyone danced beautifully, especially Dora.
She performed a special ballet piece to start
the show!

When the Dance Show was over, all the friends and family in the audience applauded. Benny gave Dora a bunch of colorful flowers. Dora liked flowers, and she really liked dancing. But most of all, she liked saving the day and making her friends happy.

SpongeBob opened his front door and greeted another beautiful Bikini Bottom morning.

"It's a perfect day," he said. "A perfect day for chores!"

SpongeBob loved to . . .

dust,

wash,

and vacuum.

"It's laundry day, Gary!" SpongeBob said.
He collected all his square pants—and even Gary's
pants, too—and filled the washing machine.

    While the clothes were drying, Patrick called.
"Hi, SpongeBob," he said. "Listen to how long
I can whistle."

SpongeBob learned that Patrick could
whistle for a long, **long**, **long** time.

Gary got his pants out of the
dryer in time, but SpongeBob waited
too long. All his pants had shrunk!

"Gary, it looks like I need to get
new pants," SpongeBob said.
Gary said, *"Meow."*

Unfortunately, the pants store at the mall was all out of SpongeBob's style! And there wasn't going to be another shipment of square pants for *months*!

"I guess I can find a new style of pants," SpongeBob said.

"Maybe."

"Nope."

179

Then SpongeBob found a pair of pants he liked. In fact, he thought they were perfect. "They hug me like my mother!"

On the way back home, SpongeBob
ran into Patrick. "Notice anything different?"
SpongeBob asked.

"Who are you?"

"I'm SpongeBob!"

Patrick thought for a moment.

"SpongeBob has **square** pants. Now leave
me alone, you mysterious stranger."

"Patrick's so full of tartar sauce," SpongeBob said to himself. "I'm still SpongeBob! It's just a different pair of pants."

But then Sandy didn't seem to recognize him, either.

"You sure look like **Mr. FancyPants**!" she said with a laugh.

SpongeBob wasn't too worried, because he knew that Patrick and Sandy could be pretty silly sometimes. But when Squidward didn't recognize him, he got scared.

(Actually, Squidward did recognize SpongeBob. He was just trying to ignore him.)

"These pants are more powerful than I
expected!" SpongeBob cried. "I guess I'm not
SpongeBob SquarePants anymore. I'll have to
start all over! I'm ready! I'm ready! I'M READY!"

The first thing SpongeBob FancyPants needed was a job. So he went to the place he knew best: the Krusty Krab.

The moment SpongeBob FancyPants walked in, Mr. Krabs told him to get to work.

"I've got the job!" SpongeBob shouted.

"SpongeBob FancyPants has never worked
here before," he said. "So you have to tell me
what to do. Teach me everything you know!"

"Hmmm," Squidward whispered to himself.
"Maybe I can get him fired. Then he'll leave
me alone."

So SpongeBob FancyPants learned to do everything around the Krusty Krab—just the way Squidward did it.

SpongeBob ignored the customers.

And he made fun
of the food.

The Krusty Krab got messier . . .
and **messier** . . . and **MESSIER!**
And Mr. Krabs got madder . . .
and **madder** . . . and **MADDER!**

"I'm used to Squidward doing a terrible job!"
Mr. Krabs yelled. "But I expect more from *you,*
Mr. SquarePants!"

"But I can't be SpongeBob SquarePants with
ROUND PANTS on!" SpongeBob cried.

"Well, take them off," Mr. Krabs said.

*"Whatever you say, Mr. Krabs!"*

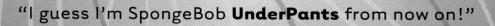
"I guess I'm SpongeBob **UnderPants** from now on!"

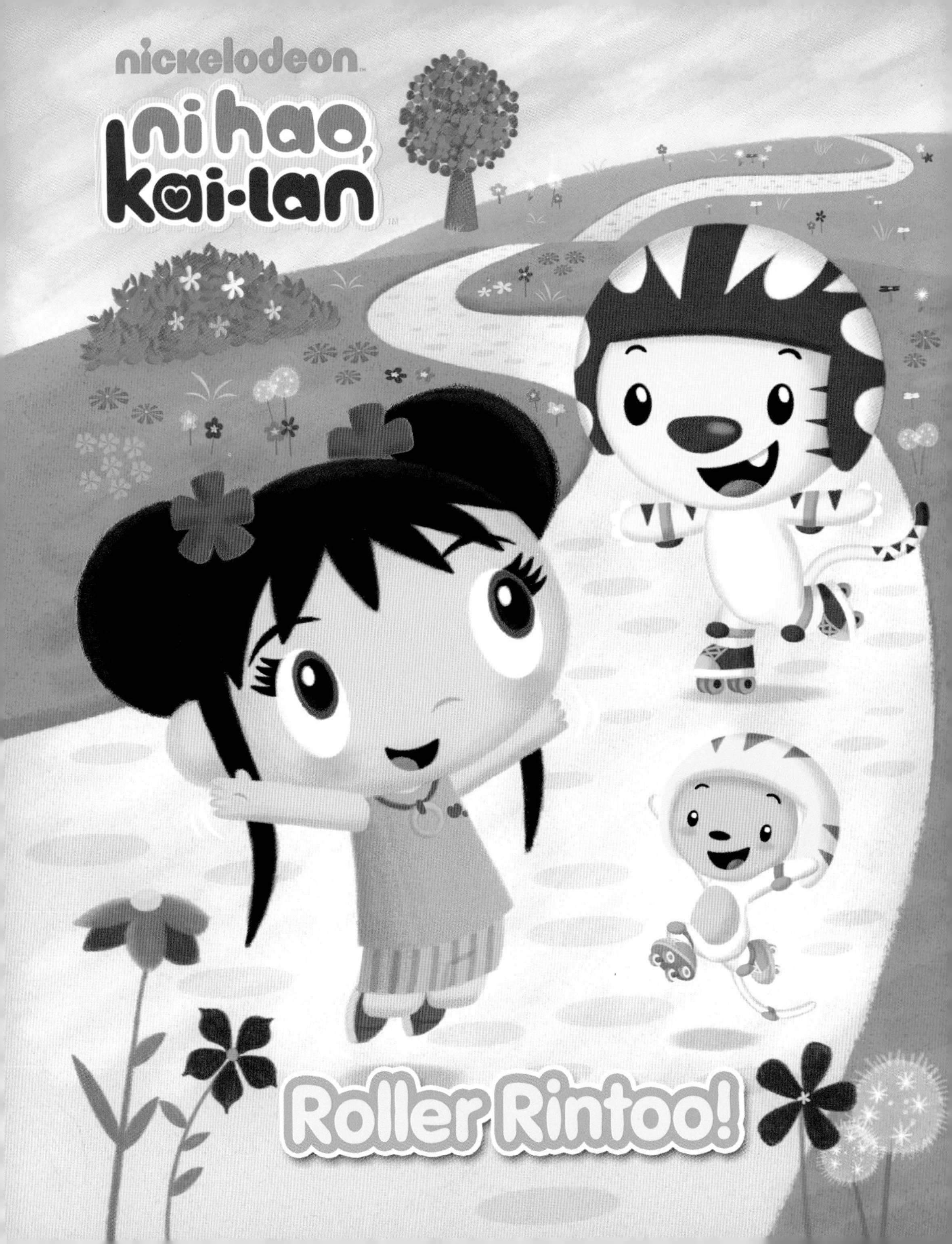
nickelodeon
ni hao, kai-lan
Roller Rintoo!

*Ni hao!* I'm Kai-lan!

Do you know what I'm doing today?
I'm putting on a helmet and pads and
my skates so I can go skating at the
roller rink! Do you like to skate?

YeYe is my grandfather. He's a great roller skater. He always helps me put on my skates and pads. *Xie xie,* YeYe.

Sometimes skating can be a little tricky.

It's a good thing YeYe is here to help.
He reminds me to start slowly.

Now I've got it! I can skate really *fast!*

Do you know how I say *fast* in Chinese? *Kuai.*

Here come Tolee and Hoho—and they're ready to skate! I really like their helmets.

We can skate uphill,

downhill,

and all around the park.

Look! There's Rintoo!

Rintoo wants to go to the roller rink, too.
He hasn't skated before,

but he's a fast runner

and a great
jumper.

He thinks skating will be easy.

Let's go, go, go to the roller rink!

Look! Lulu is on her skateboard. She's just learning, so she's going slowly and letting Mr. Fluffy and Mei Mei help her. Good luck, Lulu!

Rintoo can't wait to
put on his skates.

Do you think he's
excited to start skating?

Rintoo is ready to go.

Watch out!

It looks like skating is harder than Rintoo expected.

We want to help Rintoo, but he says he can skate by himself.

Oh, no! Rintoo threw off his skates.

Do you think he's unhappy because skating is so hard?

We were right. Rintoo wants to be a great skater, but it is really hard. What can we do to help?

I have an idea! Let's ask Lulu. She just started skateboarding by herself, and she's already really good. Let's find out how she did it.

Lulu started by going
really slowly.

Then Mei Mei and Mr. Fluffy helped her.
First with two hands . . .

then with one hand . . .

then with no hands!
Now she's a super skateboarder!

Rintoo is going to try to skate again. He's starting slowly, and Tolee and I will help.

First we'll use two hands . . .

then we'll use one hand.

Wow! Rintoo doesn't need any
more help. He can skate by himself!

He's ready to skate at the roller rink!
Great job, Rintoo! *Zhen bang!*

Wow! Rintoo's a super skater. Everyone's having a great time. The lightning bugs are here to put on a roller-rink light show!

Thank you for helping us show Rintoo how
to skate. You make my heart feel super happy.
Goodbye! *Zai jian!*